P9-CIV-901

To.. ISABEL

with a heart
full of love

Love is all around Ohio

Copyright © 2016 by Sourcebooks, Inc.
Written by Wendi Silvano
Illustrated by Joanna Czernichowska
Design by Quadrum Solutions (www.quadrumltd.com)

Sourcebooks and the colophon are registered trademarks of Sourcebooks, Inc.
All rights reserved. No part of this book may be reproduced in any form or by any electronic or
mechanical means including information storage and retrieval systems—except in the case of
brief quotations embodied in critical articles or reviews—without permission in writing from its
publisher, Sourcebooks, Inc.

Published by Sourcebooks Jabberwocky, an imprint of Sourcebooks, Inc.
P.O. Box 4410, Naperville, Illinois 60567-4410
(630) 961-3900
Fax: (630) 961-2168
www.sourcebooks.com

Source of Production: Phoenix Color, Hagerstown, Maryland
Date of Production: August 2015
Run Number: 5004410
Printed and bound in the United States of America.
PHC 10 9 8 7 6 5 4 3 2 1

Love is all around Ohio

Written by Wendi Silvano

Illustrated by Joanna Czernichowska

sourcebooks
jabberwocky

Love is a feeling that comes from **inside.**

Everyone feels it. It can't be denied.

But how do we know that it's there? What's the clue?

How can we **see** it?

Just what can we do?

Love's all around, if you just pay attention,

in people and places too many to mention.

Go look at the **park,**

on the **street,**

at the **mall.**

You'll see love all over. It's **big** and it's small!

All through **Ohio**, in cars and on trains,

in taxis and buses, on boats and on planes,

in **Akron**, and **Cleveland**,

and **Avon Lake** too,

you'll find there is **love** that will come into view.

Ohio River

Right there, on the lawn, in grand Whetstone Park

is a mom with her babe,

hearing songs of a lark.

She **swaddles** him, **cuddles** him,
kisses his ear.

That surely is **love**,
it's perfectly clear!

At a store in Columbus, a girl gets a bear.
She squeezes him,
squishes him,
ruffles his hair.

It's clear that she **loves** him. She's **smiling** and bright.

She tucks him in **softly** and **gently** at night.

That same little girl, the very next day,
sees a **friend** at her school who is too **sad** to play.

So she sits down beside him and **listens** and **shares**, making sure that he knows there's someone who **cares.**

Now the boy who was sad feels much better, you see,

so he runs home all happy to play with Magee.

They romp and they frolic.

They fetch and they run.

It's certain he loves him. They're having such fun!

You can see how **love** travels
when **shared** with a friend.
If *everyone* shares love, it never will end.
From one to another, it s p r e a d s and it grows.
You can't have *too much*, as everyone knows.

An officer in Dayton who **helps** change a flat.

A fireman in Canton who **rescues** a cat.

OHIO STADIUM

The home team that makes the crowd **cheer** and **clap**.
Each moment has **love** like a **gift** you unwrap.

There's a **father** who sits at the table each night,
helping out with the homework to get it just **right**.
He's tired and busy, but that's **love,** you know…
giving up what you want to **help** someone else **grow**.

It's not only *people* who show **love,** it's true.

Just come see the creatures

that play at the **zoo!**

The polar bear **tumbles**

and **rolls** with her cub,

and when they are finished,

she gives him a **rub.**

Where else is there **love?** Have we looked all around?

I think we've forgotten—love grows from the ground!

In the **meadows** and **gardens** and parks you will find

that the earth shows us **love** of all shapes and all kinds.

Wherever you look, **love** comes into sight.

It's there in the morning, it's there in the night.

But in all of **Ohio**,

the best love you'll find

is a **love** that is **gentle**,

and **selfless**, and **kind**...

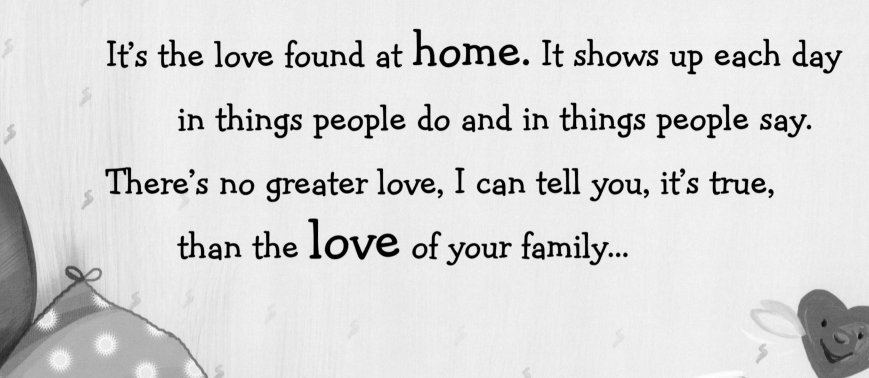

It's the love found at **home.** It shows up each day
in things people do and in things people say.
There's no greater love, I can tell you, it's true,
than the **love** of your family...

Especially for YOU!